ADAPTED BY / ADAPTADO POR
Teresa Mlawer
ILLUSTRATED BY / ILUSTRADO POR
Olga Cuéllar

Little Red Riding Hood

Caperucita Roja

Adirondack Books

Once upon a time there was a little girl who lived in a small house near the woods.

Everyone called her Little Red Riding Hood because she always wore a red hooded cape that her grandmother had made for her.

Había una vez una niña pequeña que vivía en una casita muy cerca del bosque.

Todos la llamaban Caperucita Roja porque siempre llevaba puesta una capa roja con caperuza que su abuelita le había hecho.

R0442613712

One day, Little Red Riding Hood's mother told her that her grandmother was not feeling well.

She asked Little Red Riding Hood to go to her grandmother's house and take her a jar of honey and an apple pie that she had made.

Before she left, Little Red Riding Hood's mother reminded her to be careful in the woods, and not to stop to talk to anyone so she could get to her grandmother's house quickly.

Un día, la mamá de Caperucita le dijo que la abuelita no se sentía bien.

Le pidió a Caperucita que fuera a casa de la abuelita y le llevara un tarro de miel y un pastel de manzana que ella le había hecho.

Antes de salir, la mamá de Caperucita le recordó que tuviera cuidado en el bosque y que no se detuviera a hablar con nadie para que pudiera llegar pronto a casa de la abuelita.

Little Red Riding Hood was walking in the woods very happily, when suddenly she came across a wolf that had not eaten in a long time.

"Little Red Riding Hood, where are you going with that beautiful red cape?" asked the wolf.

"I'm going to see my grandmother, who is not feeling well," said Little Red Riding Hood.

"What are you carrying in that basket?"

"I'm taking her an apple pie and a jar of honey to make her feel better."

Caperucita iba muy contenta caminando por el bosque cuando, de pronto, se encontró con un lobo, que llevaba mucho tiempo sin comer.

—Caperucita, ¿adónde vas con esa capa roja tan bonita? —le preguntó el lobo.

—Voy a ver a mi abuelita, que no se encuentra bien —contestó Caperucita.

—¿Qué llevas en esa cesta?

—Le llevo un pastel de manzana y un tarro de miel para que se mejore.

"Does your grandmother live far?"

"No, she lives on the other side of the woods."

"I know a shortcut to her house," said the wolf. "On the way, you'll find very pretty flowers and you can make a beautiful bouquet. That will surely make her happy."

"That's very nice of you, Mr. Wolf," said Little Red Riding Hood.

—¿Vive muy lejos tu abuelita?

—No, vive al otro lado del bosque.

—Conozco un atajo —dijo el lobo—. En el camino encontrarás flores muy bonitas y podrás hacerle un lindo ramo. Seguramente se pondrá contenta.

—Muy amable de su parte, señor Lobo —respondió Caperucita.

The wolf ran off so he could get to the grandmother's house before Little Red Riding Hood.

"Bang, bang," he knocked on the door.

"Who's there?" asked the grandmother from her bed.

El lobo salió corriendo para llegar antes que Caperucita a casa de la abuelita.

<<Pum, pum>>, tocó a la puerta.

—¿Quién es? —preguntó desde la cama la abuelita.

"It's me, grandma," answered the wolf, imitating the voice of Little Red Riding Hood.

"Just push open the door, it's not locked," said the grandmother.

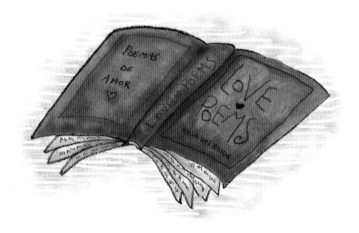

—Soy yo, abuelita —contestó el lobo, imitando la voz de Caperucita.

—Empuja la puerta, no está cerrada —dijo la abuelita.

And before you could count to three, the wolf went into the house and locked the grandmother in the closet.

He put on the grandmother's nightgown and bonnet, slipped into bed, and covered himself with the blanket.

Y en un dos por tres, el lobo entró a la casa y encerró a la abuelita en el armario.

Se puso el camisón de dormir y el gorro de la abuela, se metió en la cama y se cubrió con la manta.

A little while later, Little Red Riding Hood, holding a beautiful bouquet of flowers, knocked on the door.

"Come in, my dear granddaughter," said the wolf, imitating the grandmother's voice.

Al poco rato, Caperucita, sosteniendo un bello ramo de flores, tocó a la puerta.

—Entra, mi querida nietecita —dijo el lobo, imitando la voz de la abuelita.

Little Red Riding Hood approached the bed, and even though it seemed to her that her grandmother looked very different, she thought it was because she was not feeling well.

She took a closer look at her and said:

"Grandma, what big arms you have!"

"The better to hug you with," said the wolf.

"Grandma, what big eyes you have!"

"The better to see you with, my dear granddaughter."

Caperucita se acercó a la cama y, aunque notó a su abuelita muy cambiada, pensó que era porque no se sentía bien. La observó más detenidamente y dijo:

—Abuelita, ¡qué brazos tan grandes tienes!

—Son para abrazarte mejor —dijo el lobo.

—Abuelita, ¡qué ojos tan grandes tienes!

—Son para verte mejor, mi querida nietecita.

"Grandma, what big ears you have!"

"The better to hear you with, my darling."

"Grandma, what a big mouth you have!" said Little Red Riding Hood, very frightened.

"The better to eat you with!" cried the wolf as he jumped out of bed to catch Little Red Riding Hood.

—Abuelita, ¡qué orejas tan grandes tienes!

—Son para oírte mejor, cariño.

—Abuelita, ¡qué boca tan grande tienes! —dijo Caperucita, muy asustada.

—¡Es para comerte mejor! —gritó el lobo y saltó de la cama para atrapar a Caperucita.

But at that very moment, two hunters were passing by and heard Little Red Riding Hood's screams. They rushed into the house, captured the wolf, and took him far, far away into the woods.

Pero, justo en ese momento, pasaron dos cazadores que oyeron los gritos de Caperucita.

Entraron rápidamente a la casa, atraparon al lobo y se lo llevaron lejos, muy lejos en el bosque.

And ever since that day, Little Red Riding Hood always remembers her mother's advice, and she never strays from the path or stops to talk to anyone when she goes to visit her grandmother.

Y desde ese día, Caperucita Roja siempre recuerda los consejos de su mamá y nunca se aparta del camino ni se detiene a hablar con nadie cuando va a visitar a su abuelita.

TEXT COPYRIGHT ©2014 BY TERESA MLAWER / ILLUSTRATIONS COPYRIGHT©2014 BY ADIRONDACK BOOKS

ALL RIGHTS RESERVED. NO PART OF THIS BOOK MAY BE REPRODUCED OR TRANSMITTED IN ANY FORM OR BY ANY MEANS, ELECTRONIC OR MECHANICAL, INCLUDING PHOTOCOPYING, RECORDING OR BY ANY INFORMATION STORAGE AND RETRIEVAL SYSTEM, WITHOUT PERMISSION IN WRITING FROM THE PUBLISHER.

FOR INFORMATION, PLEASE CONTACT ADIRONDACK BOOKS, P.O. BOX 266, CANANDAIGUA, NEW YORK, 14424

ISBN 978-0-9883253-3-3   10 9 8 7 6 5 4 3 2 1   PRINTED IN CHINA